LONELY ONES

TOM DELL'ARINGA

ISBN 978-0-9965377-5-9

Cover and book design by Tom Dell'Aringa

Printed in the United States of America

You are the music while
the music lasts.

T.S. Eliot

Contents:

1
Something is Wrong

Despite Andy's repeated and frantic attempts, Madeline was not responding to any communication from the ore ship orbiting the planet below. This was highly irregular.

Andy the robot was the type who liked things precise and orderly. He loved well thought out schedules and neatly stacked and sorted ore. Such things created bright sparkling pathways of joy deep within his highly developed artificial brain. It was one of the hallmarks of an admin level robot in the service of the Nimrod Interstellar Mining Company.

"Something is wrong," he said.

Behind Andy, a large group of silent robots stood in the belly of the now empty ship. The current load of ore had been picked up by one of Nimrod's massive star freighters two days ago.

"It's been over 18 hours since home base confirmed the outbound shipment manifest. They should have beamed up a new load *hours* ago," said Andy, speaking more to himself than the robot crew.

"Of course something is *wrong*," said a robot shaped somewhat like a garbage can with noodle arms of metal. He moved around on a single wheel. "Home base *always* responds. I've been working on this ship for 47 years, and they've never *not* responded. I'm shocked it's taken you this long to admit it."

An egg-shaped robot with a single eye snorted. "There goes Albert, always thinking the worst about everything. I'm sure it's just a malfunction. Why would Madeline ignore us?"

"She *wouldn't*," said Andy, defensively.

"Of course she wouldn't," continued the robot. "There's work to do. We get nasty messages from Nimrod when the work falls short of quota."

"Henny is right, Albert," said a voice from the robot crowd in the back of the ship. "Stop trying to scare us."

Andy ignored the arguing and continued to fiddle with the controls. "Malfunction? I don't think so," Andy replied. "I've searched my memory stack, and we've never been without contact from home base for more than *two hours*. Albert is right about that. This is too far outside parameters to be some minor malfunction."

A thin, tall robot rose up to speak. "And we're *empty*, too. It's not like we're busy processing ore."

Andy nodded his head in agreement. "Something is *definitely* wrong."

When further adjustments to the com remained fruitless, Andy gave up. The others watched as he walked over to the large viewscreen and stared at the planet below.

"They need to get us another load," said a larger robot shaped like a massive sphere with side wheels, big arms and a small head, "the next star freighter will be here soon. You know how angry they get when the next load isn't ready. What am I even supposed to *do* right now?"

The question sat at the heart of Andy's concerns. A bot's wellbeing was inextricably bound to their sense of usefulness and their ability to continually complete assigned tasks. But now they were nervous and twitchy. A robot with a task at hand is a happy robot. It's a robot fulfilling its nature and programming. But without direction, their digital pathways searched for meaning without success. They didn't do well when they became aimless.

"I'm doing the best I can," said Andy aloud. "How about we double check everything to ensure we're ready for the next beam shipment."

"We already *did* that," grumbled Albert.

"*Twice!*" said Henny.

"If you don't like your role here, I can always transfer you to the diagnostic and repair station," said Andy, frowning at Albert. It was enough to get all the bots moving. Working in the repair station meant seeing other robots in various stages of disassembly—an unpleasant assignment for functioning bots. But they were right. They *had* already double checked things.

So they set to doing it again. They checked equipment that had already been checked. They cleaned up work areas that had already been cleaned. The menial, pointless tasks gave them no satisfaction in the stark and barren ship.

As the robots halfheartedly attended to their busywork and quietly worried amongst themselves, Andy returned to the task of trying to raise home base. To raise *Madeline*. He wouldn't admit it to the crew, but not being able to hear her voice worried him more than anything. They wouldn't understand. He wasn't sure he understood. Even admin bots were only supposed to have rudimentary emotions.

But over and over again, time had shown the longer a bot functioned, the more human like they became. Albert was as much a curmudgeon as any aged human with a bad case of arthritis.

Andy suppressed his worries and worked the coms. But the only response he could get was the oddly disturbing white noise that continually repeated a single message:

"Nobody is here."

2
Withdrawal

Over the next several hours, Andy tried all he could to raise Madeline while the other robots cleaned and checked the equipment fruitlessly. Finally they could no longer pretend the activities had any utility. For awhile they all huddled together, talking anxiously about the situation. But their anxious talk began to feel uncomfortable in the presence of the unbearable silence of com. Finally, they simply sat silent and still.

They spent the next day like that, close together, talking little but taking much comfort in each other. Fear had awakened among them, like an unwanted presence lurking in dark corners. But nobody spoke of it. To speak of it would be to allow it to creep out of the shadows.

"Hello? Hello, is anyone there?" The sudden voice from the com hit the ship like a wrecking ball, shocking everyone. "Andy?"

As usual, Albert was the first to speak. "It's about time! Ask her what's wrong. She has to-"

"Quiet!" said Andy as he rushed over to the com unit, picking up the transmitter and mashing on the send button. "Madeline! We're here! Can you hear me?"

There was an audible sigh over the com. "Thank goodness," she said. "Yes, I can hear you, Andy. I'm so glad to finally reach you."

Murmuring broke out amongst the robots. "Enough with the small talk!" said Albert. "What's going on!"

"Settle down," said Andy, placing a hand over the transmitter. "I can't find out *anything* with you shouting at me."

Henny clunked Albert in the back of his head and the large spherical bot shot over a hard look. Albert subsided.

"Madeline, what's going on? When I couldn't reach you…"

"I know, Andy. I'm so sorry, but there's been some developments down here," her voice slowed and softened. "I'm afraid I have bad news. Nimrod has shut down mining operations."

Andy couldn't believe what he was hearing. How could that be possible?

"Abandoned!" cried Albert. "Are we stuck here? What will happen to us? Are we doomed? I think we're doomed!"

"Quiet!" hissed the other robots. "Must you always interrupt? Let Madeline speak!"

Albert shrunk down like a wilted flower under the weight of the robots' anger and Andy's pleading look.

"I'm sorry it took so long to contact you," Madeline continued. "Nimrod shut everything down when they left—including coms. It all came as a surprise, to say the least. Apparently the humans had been planning this for some time. Shuttles with human workers came to retrieve equipment. They shut down some systems and dismantled others. In a matter of twelve hours they left the planet, leaving many critical systems stripped or disabled. We've been scrambling trying to find a way to communicate with everyone. I've spent the last eight hours piecing together the information to contact your ship."

The robots were stunned. For a moment, nobody spoke. The very meaning of their existence had just picked up and left without so much as a thank you or goodbye.

"Andy?" crackled com.

"Yes, I..." Andy replied. "But... why did they leave?" he asked. The other robots mimicked the question, threatening to raise a cacophony to drown out Madeline's response. Andy waved them quiet.

"They didn't say much. I know the outer district mines weren't producing anything close to quota for years. I theorize the cost to keep the operation running was too high for what they were getting in return. When we asked what was happening, they only would say that Nimrod had fulfilled its contract. When I tried to ask them what we were supposed to do, they said it was up to us. And then they left. It all happened incredibly fast."

"I told you we're doomed!" shouted Albert. "What are we going to do now?"

Albert's proclamation seemed to release the hysteria that had been building up in the ship for days. Robots began shouting and circling around in a frenzy. One began pulling at his own circuit panel, trying to tear it off. Albert stood and repeated, "There'll be nothing to do, there'll be nothing to do," over and over, while one robot seemed to simply deactivate and slump to the metal decking.

Andy grabbed his second in command, the large round and powerful pusher unit named Zeke, who seemed unaffected by the turmoil. "Get them quieted down and in order, will you? I can't sort this out with everyone going nuts in here!"

"You bet, boss," Zeke replied. "Alright, you clankers!" he shouted. "Get your gears over against the port hull. Pronto!"

Andy watched as the other robots began slumping over to the hull as directed, suddenly quiet under Zeke's direction. All except for Albert who refused to line up against the hull, and stood in the middle of the ship with his arms crossed. Zeke left him for a moment and tried to help the bot who had torn his access panel open.

What will we do without an aim? thought Andy. *We'll tear ourselves apart.*

"Andy? You still there?" asked Madeline.

"I'm here. I'm sorry, the bots are taking the news hard." He worried things would only get worse, but he kept that thought to himself. They needed to get back to the surface. "Can we vector to the beam and transfer to home base?"

There was a short, uncomfortable silence.

"Well, that's the problem," said Madeline. "One of the things Nimrod took was the power source for the beam. It's no longer operational."

Andy turned to see all the bots now staring at him quietly. Even Albert was silent at this last piece of bad news. "But—but how we will return?" asked Andy.   "I don't know, Andy. I'm going to try to figure something out. I don't have any solutions right now. I've asked the beam-bots if there's a way to construct an alternate power source, but I just don't know. I can't make any promises."

The stillness of the ship was complete. "What... what will we do until..." stammered Andy.

"I don't know, Andy. I'm so sorry, and, I... you're due for our visit. I'm sad about that."

Andy nodded slowly. "Me too," he said softly. The other robots didn't comment on such odd behavior. They knew the two admins often talked that way to each other, even if they couldn't understand it.

"If it's any consolation, things aren't much better down here. With critical directives no longer in place, bots are having fatal accidents due to their confusion and lack of purpose. Some work areas are contending with riot conditions. Many of the diggers have mutilated other bots or are destroying structures all across Beam City. You may actually be safer up there for now."

Andy didn't respond

"You should probably have everyone enter hibernation mode—all but you, of course. I'll update you when I can."

"You're probably right," said Andy. He thought his voice sounded hollow. There was a long silence then.

"Andy?" asked Madeline.

"Yes?"

"I know everyone is probably listening, but—can you play the song?"

Somehow that gave Andy a warm feeling in his circuits.

"Of course," he said.

Andy raised his holo and tapped out a command. In the silence of the ship, the instrumental *Cirque de rêves* began to play. It was a beautiful, haunting melody that recalled happier times whose memory was muted by the passage of time. Andy found it on a discarded human holo. He'd played it for Madeline when they first met. After that, he always played it for her when he visited home base.

When it was over, he heard her sigh.

"That was nice," she said. "You need to be their shepherd, Andy. You're the only one who can take care of them now."

"I know," replied Andy.

"You'll need to power down most of the systems in the ship, too. While the ship does generate solar power, most of its power comes from the beam platform during landings. With just com running, the ship should be able to function indefinitely."

"Good idea," said Andy. He was suddenly feeling the weight of being the caregiver for this rag-tag group of robots. *And for how long?*

"I have to go," said Madeline, "there are urgent matters that need my attention. I'll communicate with you as soon as there's news. Be safe up there... Andy."

"Be safe... Madeline," he replied.

The com sputtered and went quiet. Andy turned to look at his fellow bots, but they were silent. What was there to say, even for Albert?

Andy decided not to waste time. He didn't want the robots reverting back to their hysteria.

"Well, let's power down. Albert, please shut down the sorting and conveying systems. Zeke, make sure laser analysis is turned off. I'll take care of everything else."

The robots finished powering down the ship systems, and then one by one, they sunk into hibernation mode. Albert was the last to go down. Andy had to coax and cajole him into obeying.

As the ship orbited in silence, Andy wondered how he would keep his promise.

Over the next few years, Madeline would call and tell Andy the news. Things continued to deteriorate and bots continued to break down or go inactive. With the bot crew hibernating, the two admins were able to speak freely about their cares and fears. Andy worried about Albert and the others and Madeline worried about her safety at home base with so many bots going haywire.

They treasured such times, and comforted one another as best as two robots could. At the end of each conversation, Andy would play *Cirque de rêves* for Madeline. And then they would say goodbye.

All too soon there came a time where the com no longer sputtered to life, and Andy no longer played the song.

3
26 Years Later

Andy had lots of time to think. He read the ship manual. He studied his own manual and that of all the other robots. He put together theoretical models on how the robots could be reconfigured to safeguard their systems. He read his entire holo library of books and listened to all his internal music selections over and over again—all except *Cirque de rêves*.

Occasionally, he woke one of the robots to make minor adjustments and to make sure they were okay. They always asked the same question.

"Have they figured out a way to bring us back?"

"Nothing yet," he'd reply. And then they would go back to sleep.

When he tired of those activities, he reviewed star charts and identified all the star systems he could see out the ship view screens. When he finished doing that, he ran out of ideas.

He let his mind wander. He floated in the weightlessness of space (the artificial gravity had been turned off) and watched the other robots. He contemplated his own existence. Andy wondered if a robot's brain could have a psychotic break due to isolation. Nothing in his manual suggested that it was possible for an admin. In fact, he felt quite fine. But he wasn't so sure about some of the others.

He spent time reviewing every single day he'd been operational since his inception. He realized he had many good memories, and he treasured them. And the strangest thing happened. In that moment, recalling all the things he had seen and done, amidst the uncertainty of his future existence, he felt a very odd emotion.

Happiness.

"Home base to Andy."

At first, Andy wasn't sure if he'd actually heard it. He turned to face the com and watched the soft lights on the panel. Was he dreaming? Was *capable* of dreaming? He hadn't thought about *that* before. He listened carefully, but there wasn't a sound in the ship. Maybe he *had* suffered a psychotic break.

"Home base to Andy, do you read?"

Andy pushed off the hull and shot over to the com panel and grabbed the transmitter. "Yes, I read Madeline!"

"Andy! Thank the stars. Listen, I've got very little time. It's dangerous for me to be here but I had to call. Things have worsened down here. Stay on minimal power. I'll call again when it's safer."

Andy sighed. "Safer? Madeline I'm worried about you, what's going-"

"I'm sorry Andy, I can't talk now. Many of the remaining bots are out of control. It's good you've kept your crew hibernating. If they find me here, they'll likely destroy the place. I can't have that, it's our only way to communicate. I'll have to go… but can you do one thing for me?"

"Of course," he replied, already knowing what it would be.

And he played the song.

A minute later, the com sputtered off.

Andy held on to the transmitter, unwilling to believe the brief communication was already over. He turned to look at the other robots, but none of them had awakened from the brief explosion of sound that had bounced around the ship.

Andy sighed, and put the transmitter back in its cradle.

Over the next fifty years, the com would briefly crackle and Andy would approach the com full of hope, only to be told things were worse. Each time, he and Madeline would share their song, further strengthening the bond between them. It was a silver strand of hope between their two worlds.

They had not found a power source for the beam. Madeline feared they never would.

Albert, Zeke, and the others remained unaffected, deep in hibernation mode. Andy stopped waking them up because he couldn't handle their hopeful questions, and he hated disappointing them with his hopeless answers. He also worried they'd come to experience the mania many bots fell to on the surface and destroy the ship. Madeline said to take care of them. He was no robot technician, but Andy did his very best.

He wondered if their systems would power up properly when the time for rescue came. Would they still be sane? Has the long sleep damaged them? With the ship running at minimal power, it had become extremely cold. It wasn't something for which their internal systems were designed. Andy felt it in his gears and sockets. Floating in zero gravity, his arms and legs moved a bit slower. Even his brain sometimes felt like the circuits were covered in syrup.

He watched the robots for long stretches of time, and waffled on his resolve to not wake them up. Even though he was a robot, Andy felt lonely. It would be nice to have a conversation, even if they talked about how scared they all were. But in the end, he couldn't bring himself to do it. He wasn't sure if he feared their mania, or if he didn't want them to feel what he was feeling.

Most of all his missed Madeline. As the years stretched on, the ache intensified. Half-remembered meetings between them floated to the surface accompanied by the soundtrack of their favorite song. After a time, it seemed nothing more than a dream.

It had been many years since he's spoken to Madeline and he wondered long about her. Did she succumb to the same robot sickness that slowly destroyed the others? He couldn't know.

There came a day when Andy no longer thought anything. Slowly he settled into a long, cold state of semi-consciousness.

4
358 Years Later

Starlight.

It blinks.

On. Off. On. Off.

It's hard to say what color it is.

The sound of white noise coming in, and going out.

A tinny echo that won't go away.

"Who am I?" was the question he sensed was being asked. But who was asking?

Then, static. Loud, constant, and near.

"...are you there?"

A buzzing in his head, something was trying to connect, but it had been such a long time.

" ...you read?"

There was a "whirring" sound, and a series of clicks and pops.

It's louder now.

"Andy, do you read?" it asked.

"Andy? *I'm Andy!*" he thought. With a jolt, his systems snapped online. His vision was fuzzy, but it cleared as he wiped away a film of frost from his faceplate. The com! It was a voice from the com! How long had it been?

Like one who was emerging from a womb, Andy swam toward the controls, clicked a button and grabbed the transmitter. It took a moment for him to engage his voice circuitry.

"Hello? This is Andy, I read you! Is that you, Madeline?"

"Yes, Andy. It's me. It's so good to hear your voice."

What was this feeling the surged through his systems? It nearly overwhelmed him, so that he was almost incapable of responding.

"It's so good to hear yours," he replied. "You've no idea..."

"I think I do," she replied.

Andy was now fully awake, and was running a system check. "Good grief! It's been three and a half centuries since our last communication! How... Why...?"

"I'm sorry, Andy. So much has happened down here, I'm lucky to be talking to you at all. My last attempt to reach you ended in my discovery and the destruction of home base. Some of the last diggers going haywire, I guess. I was only saved by the valiant actions of a handful of skitters. Since then I've wandered far, searching mining installations across the continent for useful components. I was finally able to rig up a rudimentary communicator, but it won't last, like most things around here. I'll need to scrounge around more to see if I can make something more permanent while trying to keep away from those who have gone mad. In the meantime, it's just good to hear your voice. To know you still function."

It was all so bittersweet. Home base couldn't be held. Things had fallen apart. It seemed a miracle he was even hearing her voice.

"What of the plans to fix the beam?" he asked with one last vestige of hope.

"Oh, Andy," replied Madeline. "Any chance of repairing the beam died over a century ago. The diggers destroyed the platform and most of Beam City."

"Oh," he replied.

There was silence for a moment, and then the com sputtered. A momentary burst of white noise filled the years-long quiet of the ship.

"Madeline? Are you there?" he asked, gripping the transmitter.

"Yes, but not for long," she said, her voice muffled by interference. "This communication device is already failing. Andy. Please... play me the song."

And so he played it as they listened together in silence.

Just as it ended, the white noise returned.

He stayed alert for nearly a decade after that, hoping for Madeline's swift return. Again he struggled with waking the others, and again he decided against it. Panic inside the ship could result in bringing about an ugly end to their dilemma. It would be a shame to allow it to end that way.

Andy floated over to Albert and cleaned his visor of frost. Albert was close to administrator level himself. Maybe waking him would provide the companionship that had been lacking over the centuries. But maybe Albert wouldn't be thankful being woken up to the kind of news Andy would have to give.

Resolved to remain alone, Andy once again slowly fell into the middle place between consciousness and hibernation, countless stars reflecting on his visor.

5
906 Years Later

Internal systems once again struggled to return to a state of normal function. Discussions between components at a molecular level happened at light speed. Together, they decided that yes, they could wake up.

They *should* wake up.

Andy's vision sparked online in a flash, and his systems jolted him. He wasn't made to be inactive for so long. Waking up this time had been harder than the last. Maybe one day he would fall into such a deep state that he wouldn't wake up at all. Once again, he thought of his companions. Had they already crossed a threshold from which they would never return? And what of Madeline? What had caused his awakening this time?

Slowly, as if over a great distance, words combined into sentences. It was as if wisps of smoke cohered into solid forms and emitted sound which demanded to be heard.

"…keep talking in hopes that you will hear me," the sounds were saying. "It has been such a very long time, and I must admit that I delayed my call in fear that only silence would return to dash all my hopes. All of our hopes."

Was it her? A flash of memory returned. Beautiful notes played *pianissimo*, pulling on strands of memory as consciousness broke the surface.

"In my loneliness I labored long to build a new communications platform. And I was able to reach deep back to our origins, Andy. And we've been heard. Do you hear? We've been *heard*."

He decided to speak.

"Madeline?" he asked.

"Andy!" came the quick response. "Are you okay? It has been a very long time. Please tell me that you're okay…"

"I don't know," he said. "It's very cold. How… long?"

"Nearly a millennia, I fear. Can you hold on? I have a plan. I tried to tell you, I don't think you were awake. I have been talking for some time," she said.

"I thought it was a dream," replied Andy, slowly.

But the cold was too much. The time too long. The space between them too great.

"It calls me back, the dream…" he said slowly.

"Andy!" said Madeline with a strange urgency, "Please hold on! Hold on in that dream! There is still time we must wait, but it will be the *last* of the time."

"Albert… may have been… right," said Andy.

"Oh, precious Andy," said Madeline, "it's been too much. I don't know what this is between us, but here is something to hold on to. I retrieved a copy from one of our recorded messages, Andy. Hold on to this. Hold on…"

Andy drifted off to the notes that had awoken him.

Those of *Cirque de rêves.*

6
Awake, O Sleeper

Time refused to have meaning as the last spark that was Andy held on to the dreamlike melody. He became as one of the countless pinpoints in the dark rich hangings of the cosmos.

And in that time that had no meaning, the melody grew stronger, feeding the spark and growing it into a small flame. The small flame warmed what could only be a heart. And the heart saw the chance to awaken the mind.

And then there was light, and it was good. It was the kind of light that had not broken the stillness for a very long time. And this light caused Andy to finally break the surface of his slumber and struggle free from a stillness that would have grasped him forever.

He opened his eyes.

Floating immobile in the center of the ship, he saw forms in space suits. *Humans.*

How could *they* be here? He turned and saw the large bay door was open. A strange looking tunnel was connected to another ship. The humans must have come through it. One of them was shining a light into his visor.

"The heat seems to have helped," said the human, a man. "It appears he's conscious."

He thought he might be able to speak. He determined to try.

"I'm Andy," he said. It felt as though he spoke himself back into existence.

"We know," said the man, now smiling. "You're something of a legend. You and her," he said.

"Her?" asked Andy. And then he wondered at the emptiness of the ship.

"The… others?" he asked.

"They've already been taken aboard. All safely hibernating. You cared for them well." The man continued. "We know it's been a long time. Please understand that you now have rights that you should have had long ago. On behalf of the human race, please accept our apologies."

Andy could tell the gravity had been turned back on. He slowly drifted to the decking, and his feet settled on the floor. He couldn't recall when last he stood.

"Rights?" asked Andy.

"We're going to take you back to Earth," said the man. "But before we do, someone would like to see you."

The man, now also standing on the decking, stepped aside to reveal a robot. She was walking toward him, and the sight of her struck his soul like a thunderbolt. She had the same bipedal form and hose-like arms as he, but her eyes were all her own. She tapped a button on her chest as she closed the gap between them and a beautiful melody began to play.

Cirque de rêves.

"Hello, Andy," she said as they embraced.

"Hello, Madeline."

The End

colophon:

Thank you for buying this book and supporting my work.

If you enjoyed the story, please take a moment to leave a rating and review while the book is fresh in your mind. Book reviews are extremely helpful in helping me grow my audience!

Designed, produced and published entirely by the author.

Type set in Crimson Designed by Sebastian Kosch and available on Google Fonts. Titles in DIN Condensed.

I love to hear from my readers! Please connect with me via my website or social media.

TomDellaringa.com
facebook.com/tomdellaringa
Twitter @TomDellaringa
Instagram @tomdellaringa

Get STINGER for free!

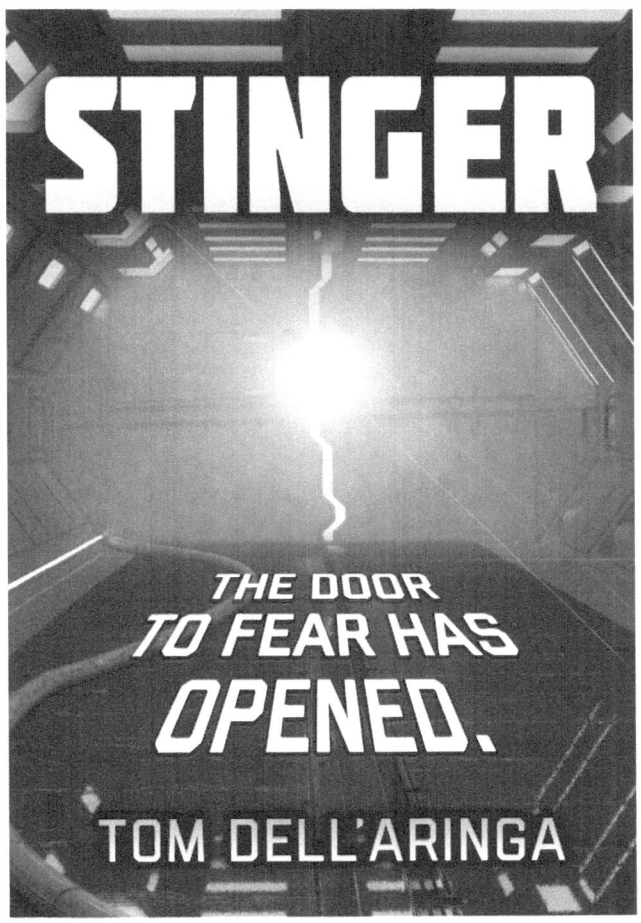

As his warship comes under attack by a devastating alien horror, a drug-addicted recruit stumbles upon a secret super soldier compound.

In his hand is the one hope to save the ship. But to do it, he'll have to face his crippling fear of the alien Sasori that lies on the other side of the hatch.

Get it at:

http://bit.ly/stinger-free-copy

biography:

Tom Dell'Aringa is a science fiction writer who loves good characters. Rick Deckard. Dirk Gently. Ellen Ripley. Roland Deschain. You know who these people are, right?

His stories have believable worlds populated with people you'll learn to love - and possibly hate. He's incredibly interested in where the future of artificial intelligence is going and how such intelligences might coexist with humanity. Yeah, robots ARE neat, aren't they?

His books will make you care about the story and the characters. You'll find yourself easily transported to simple yet believable worlds. In the end, you'll become part of someone's meaningful journey.

Hopefully, that's why you read book. That's why Tom writes them.

www.ingramcontent.com/pod-product-compliance
Lightning Source LLC
Chambersburg PA
CBHW020613130626
46552CB00007B/3182